I SURVIVED

HURRICANE KATRINA, 2005

I SURVIVED

THE SINKING OF THE *TITANIC*, 1912

THE SHARK ATTACKS OF 1916

HURRICANE KATRINA, 2005

HURRICANE KATRINA, 2005

by Lauren Tarshis

illustrated by Scott Dawson

Scholastic Inc.

NEW YORK   TORONTO   LONDON   AUCKLAND

SYDNEY   MEXICO CITY   NEW DELHI   HONG KONG

ISBN 978-0-545-20696-9

25 24   13 14 15 16/0

Printed in the U.S.A.   40
First printing, March 2011
Designed by Tim Hall

FOR JEREMY

CHAPTER 1

MONDAY, AUGUST 29, 2005
7:00 A.M.
THE LOWER NINTH WARD,
NEW ORLEANS, LOUISIANA

Hurricane Katrina was ripping apart New Orleans, and eleven-year-old Barry Tucker was lost and alone, clinging to an oak tree for dear life. He'd fallen off the roof of his house and been swept away in the floodwater. The raging current had tossed and twisted him, almost tearing him to pieces. He would have drowned, but somehow Barry had grabbed hold of the tree. With every bit of strength in his body, he'd pulled himself out of the water and wrapped his arms and legs around the trunk.

Now he was holding on, with no idea what to do next.

Wind howled around him. Rain hammered down. And all Barry could see was water. Swirling, foaming, rushing water. The water had washed away his whole neighborhood. Pieces of it floated by. In the dirty gray light, Barry saw jagged hunks of wood, shattered glass, a twisted bicycle, a refrigerator, a stuffed penguin, a mattress covered with a pink blanket. He tried hard not to imagine what else was in that water or what had happened to all his neighbors . . . and his mom and dad and little sister, Cleo.

What if they'd all fallen into the water too? What if . . .

Wait! What was that sound? Was someone calling his name?

"Dad!" Barry screamed. "Mom! Cleo!"

No. It was just the wind shrieking. Even the sky was terrified of this storm.

Barry was shaking now. Tears stung his eyes. And then he heard a new sound, a cracking and groaning, above the wind and rain. He stared in shock at what was floating in the water.

A house.

Or what was left of it. One side was torn off. It moved through the flood slowly, turning. Its blown-out windows seemed to stare at Barry. The splintered wood looked like teeth in a wide-open mouth.

And it was coming right at him.

CHAPTER 2

TWENTY-ONE HOURS EARLIER
SUNDAY, AUGUST 28, 2005
10:00 A.M.
THE TUCKERS' HOUSE,
THE LOWER NINTH WARD,
NEW ORLEANS, LOUISIANA

Barry sat on the steps of his front porch. His best friend, Jay, huddled next to him. Jay wanted to see the drawing rolled up in Barry's hands.

"Show me!" Jay said, leaning so close Barry could smell egg sandwich on his breath.

Barry elbowed him back, laughing. He knew Jay was excited. They both were.

The next day was the deadline for Acclaim Comic Books' "Create a Superhero" contest. For the past three weeks, Barry and Jay had been working nonstop on their creation. They'd come up with everything together — their hero's name, his costume, even his secret star, which was the source of his amazing powers. But it had been Barry's job to draw him. He'd stayed up past midnight the last three nights, adding his finishing touches.

"Okay," Barry said, clearing his throat and standing up like an announcer facing an anxious crowd. "This is the moment you've been waiting for. Ladies and gentlemen, meet Akivo!"

He unrolled the paper and watched Jay's eyes get wider behind his scratched-up glasses.

Barry's cheeks heated up. He'd worked hard

on the drawing. Of course he'd never admit it to Jay, but it was almost like Akivo was his brother. A seven-foot-tall brother with bulging muscles, hawk wings, titanium armor, and eyes that could see through walls.

Jay rose to his feet. "That's amazing," he said in a shocked whisper. "The wings look real. And that fire . . ." He pointed to the flames coming out of Akivo's silver boots. Barry had worked for three hours on those flames, mixing orange and red and yellow with a bit of blue until they looked like they would burn your fingers if you touched them.

They both stood there for a minute, staring at the drawing.

Then Jay started jumping up and down.

"We're going to win the contest!" Jay yelled. "We're going to win the contest!"

Barry started jumping too. He knew that hundreds of people were entering, and not only kids. Some people drew on computers. Others made videos. All Barry had were the colored pencils Mom and Dad had bought him for his last birthday.

Still, Barry was a believer. He had gotten that from his mom. And at that minute, Barry let himself believe that he and Jay just might win first place — $250 to split and the comic book, starring Akivo, that Acclaim would create. Barry and Jay loved comic books. They'd been collecting them since they'd learned to read.

"We're going to be rich!" Jay sang.

"And famous!" said Barry.

They were so busy jumping and dancing and hooting, they didn't notice Abe Mackay and his killer dog, Cruz, watching from the sidewalk. Abe's laughter got their attention. Abe was a huge guy — almost twice the size of Barry. His booming laugh practically shook the ground.

Barry and Jay froze. The hairs on Barry's arms stood up straight. Jay's cocoa skin turned gray.

Abe was in middle school, just a year older

than Barry and Jay. They used to all be friends. But Abe had changed since his dad had gone away two years earlier. Now he and his grandma lived alone. The Mackays' house used to be one of the nicest in their neighborhood. It was painted bright sky blue. Abe's grandma used to have a yard full of flowers you could smell a block away. But now the garden was dead and the house was gloomy. Abe didn't go to school much anymore, and he'd started hanging around the older boys whose *vroom*ing motorcycles kept everyone up at night.

And then there was his new dog. He looked like a big mutt. He had a square head, and the tips of his pointy ears flopped over. But Abe said that he was a special breed from Asia, trained by the Chinese army, and that his jaw was strong enough to bite through metal. "He's trained to kill," Abe had bragged. "On my command. He goes right for the neck. One bite is all it takes."

"Why'd you stop dancing?" Abe asked now, spitting onto the sidewalk. "Cruz loves to dance!"

He bent down to unhook the dog's leash.

"Go!" Abe shouted. "Go get 'em, Cruz!"

CHAPTER 3

Barry turned and put his hands over his face, bracing for the feeling of teeth ripping at his neck. But nothing happened.

He peeled open his eyes and saw that Cruz was still on his leash, standing next to Abe, who was laughing his head off.

Why did he think it was so funny to scare them? Barry wished he could find the courage to step forward and say, "Get off my property!"

He'd practiced that in the bathroom mirror, squinting his eyes to get a fierce look.

But who was Barry kidding? He was about as fierce as one of Mom's peanut butter cookies.

If only Barry was more like his father. Nothing ever got to Roddy Tucker.

And then, as though Barry's thoughts had sent out an SOS, the front door opened and Dad appeared on the porch.

"Hello there, Abraham," he said with a smile.

Abe pulled Cruz closer and lost his usual *what are you looking at?* glare. Suddenly he looked like the old Abe, the pudgy guy in the Saints jersey who tried to show Barry and Jay how to shoot layups.

Dad had that effect on people. He could smile at a T. rex, and next thing, they'd be making plans to have a burger together. Barry's dad was a little famous in the Lower Nine: His band, Roddy Tucker and the Blasters, played in jazz clubs around New Orleans. But Mom said that wasn't why people respected him.

"Your father's got sweet music in his heart," Mom always said. "And everyone can hear it."

Now Dad looked at Barry. "We're leaving in an hour," he said. "You need to pack up. That hurricane's getting nasty. It looks like it might be a direct hit on the city. We're leaving town."

Barry stared at Dad. Leaving town for a hurricane? Not the Tuckers! Never before. Every year a few storms fixed their sights on New Orleans, and they always petered out at the last minute. There hadn't been a bad hurricane in New Orleans in forty years.

Was Dad making this up to get Abe to hustle on home?

"I'm serious," Dad said, reading Barry's doubtful look. "There's a mandatory evacuation. First time in New Orleans history."

"What's that?" Jay asked.

"It means if you can leave, you've got to leave,"

12

Dad said. "Your mom already called, Mr. Jay. You're heading up to Birmingham."

"What about us?" Barry asked.

"Houston," Dad answered with a sorry smile.

Barry groaned. He loved Mom's Texas cousins, but all of them, five wild little girls and their grumpy mama, lived in a tiny little house. Barry always went home with a whopper headache after visiting them. Dad too. The hurricane must be bad to get Mom and Dad to head to Houston.

Barry looked around his neighborhood—the little houses, the scraggly lawns surrounded by chain-link fences, the palm trees and big oaks. He and Jay used to pretend that those big oak trees were ancient creatures rising from the earth's core.

There were better neighborhoods in New Orleans, and sometimes Mom and Dad talked about moving to a block where police cars weren't always blaring their sirens, where Mom would feel safe walking after it got dark. But the Tucker family had been on this block in the Lower Nine for seventy years. Gramps had helped his daddy build this house back when folks kept hogs in their backyards. Barry couldn't walk half a block without someone shouting hello from a porch and waving him up for a chat and a glass of iced tea.

The Lower Nine was home. And that was that.

Abe started to slink away.

"They're opening up the Superdome, Abraham," Dad called after him. "For folks without cars. You should get your grandma over to the stadium soon as you can."

Abe waved and went on his way.

Dad opened the door to go inside, and the news playing on the radio echoed out to the porch.

"That's right," a man's voice boomed. "This storm is a monster. It's time to leave. Get out now. Get out while you can!"

"You heard the man," Dad said, starting to close the door behind him. "Time to get moving."

CHAPTER 4

Barry's stomach did a few nervous flips. The news reports had been warning about Hurricane Katrina for days, but nobody in Barry's house had been paying much attention. Dad and his band had been playing shows in Atlanta. Mom worked full-time at Cleo's preschool. She also had a little business baking cookies for restaurants in the French Quarter, the fancy neighborhood across the canal. As for Barry, he was totally focused on

Akivo. A tornado could have sucked up the house and he wouldn't have noticed.

But now Barry's mind started swirling.

Like everyone in New Orleans, he understood what could happen if a strong hurricane struck. The city was surrounded by water. The Industrial Canal was just two blocks from their house. Big Lake Pontchartrain was up north. The Mississippi River wormed through the middle of the city. And so many canals and channels jutted this way and that, Barry couldn't keep track of them all. Of course there were levees — big walls of dirt and concrete that protected the city from all that water. But some people said that the levees weren't strong enough for a really big storm.

Barry thought of Hurricane Betsy, the storm that hit New Orleans the year before Dad was born. When Gramps was alive, he'd loved telling Betsy stories. He and Gran lived in this same house. The levee broke, and the Lower Nine flooded. Four feet of water filled the living room.

It had taken six months to get everything cleaned up. But Gramps was always proud of how the house held up to the winds.

"Barely lost a roof shingle," he liked to say as he patted the wall like you'd pat the back of a loyal friend.

Those Betsy stories had fascinated Barry when he was little. But they'd always seemed like ghost stories and fairy tales, stories that could never come true.

Now he wondered. . . .

"Barry!" Jay said, waving his hands in front of Barry's face. "Snap out of it!"

"Sorry!" said Barry, shaking himself out of his thoughts.

"What about Akivo?"

They had planned to walk to the post office after school tomorrow and send their package to Acclaim's offices in New York City. Barry had visited New York with Dad the past summer. The president of a famous college there was always inviting Dad to give talks about New Orleans jazz.

"I'll mail him tomorrow," Barry said. "From Houston."

"Let me have him," Jay said, holding out his hand. "I'll mail him from Birmingham."

They stared at each other without budging, until finally Jay blinked.

That settled that. Barry won the stare-out, so he got to mail Akivo.

"Don't let anything happen to him," Jay said.

"I wouldn't!"

They stood there, like they always did before they had to say good-bye. No matter how much time they spent together, it always felt like there was one more idea to talk about, one more joke to tell before they went their own ways.

"Barry, honey, we've got to get ready!" Mom called.

It was time.

Jay raised his hand toward the sky, his pinky

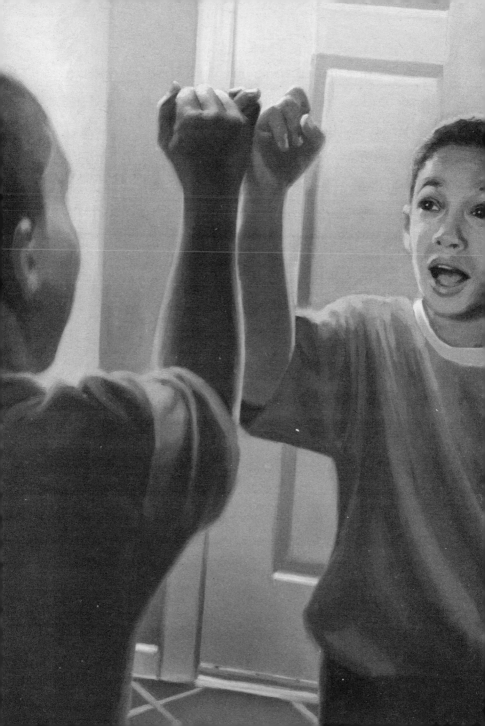

pointing up. It took Barry a few seconds to recognize the special move they'd invented for Akivo so the energy from his secret power star, Beta Draconis, could flow from his pinky into his heart.

Barry raised his hand too, and he and Jay linked their pinkies together in the air.

Barry smiled. For just a few seconds, Barry the believer imagined that he had a power star of his own somewhere.

CHAPTER 5

"Hurricane Katrina is now a Category Five storm, folks," said the man on the radio. "That's the strongest there is. Winds a hundred and seventy-five miles an hour. Waves will be twenty feet high. It's aiming right for our beautiful city. Right for us. This is the storm we've been fearing. It's time to leave. Time to get —"

Mom switched off the radio. "Okay," she said softly. "I heard you. We're leaving."

"Who are you talking to, Mom?" Barry asked.

She looked surprised to see him. "Sorry, baby!" she said, turning and kissing Barry on the cheek. "That man is getting on my nerves." She had three coolers arranged on the floor and was filling them with food for their car trip.

"Are you worried?" Barry asked, brushing some flour from Mom's sleeve. She'd been baking all morning.

"Not at all," she said, but Barry could see she was fibbing. Mom always baked when she got nervous. And she'd packed enough muffins and cookies in those coolers to feed the Saints.

"We're almost ready, right?" she asked.

Barry nodded. He'd helped Dad board up the windows. He'd carried the porch furniture and Cleo's princess house into the shed. "Need anything else?"

"Find your sister," Mom said. "She hasn't been herself all morning. I need you to work some Barry magic on her."

Barry found his sister crying in her bed.

"What is it, Clee?" he asked.

"My princess house!" she wailed. "That lady took it!"

"What lady?"

"Katrina!"

Barry tried not to smile. In that three-year-old brain of Cleo's, Katrina was probably a big fat vampire lady flying through the air.

"Your princess house is safe in the shed," Barry said. "And Katrina isn't a lady. It's just a bunch of clouds. We're not afraid of clouds, are we?"

Cleo looked at Barry with her huge teary eyes. Barry always got a soft feeling in his heart, like the purring of a little cat, when he looked at his sister. Good thing he wasn't a superhero. One look at a crying Cleo and all his powers would be drained away.

"We're having an adventure!" Barry said. "You can't cry on an adventure!"

Cleo gave a big sniff.

"Will Akivo be there?" she asked.

Of course Cleo knew all about Akivo. For weeks, anytime Barry told Cleo a bedtime story, he made Akivo the star. Who rescued Snow White from the evil stepmother? Akivo! Who saved the three little pigs from the big bad wolf? Akivo!

Now Barry put his face closer to his sister's. "I think Akivo will be waiting for us in Houston tonight," he said. He hated tricking Cleo, but it wasn't really a lie. Akivo was always appearing in Barry's dreams. Maybe Cleo would dream about him too.

"To retect us?"

"That's right," Barry said. "He will protect us."

Cleo gave another big, messy sniff and then nodded bravely. "I won't cry," she whispered.

She held out her arms so Barry could pick her up. He pulled her close. She put her head on his shoulder and let him carry her to the car.

Ten minutes later, they were on the road.

CHAPTER 6

They sped through the Lower Nine and crossed
the St. Claude Avenue Bridge. They drove past
the bakery where Mom had worked before Cleo
was born. She'd learned how to make Barry's
favorite caramel cake there. Mom's dream was
to open her own bakery. They didn't have the
money for that now. *But one day,* Mom always
said. *One day.* She said those words so often they
had become the Tucker family motto.

One day Barry's dad would have a deal with a record label.

One day they'd get rid of their dented old Honda and buy a nice new car.

Maybe even one day Barry wouldn't be so scared of Abe Mackay and his friends.

One day.

They drove a few more blocks, and then Dad pulled up in front of Lightning's, the club where he and his band played most Thursday nights. The owner, Dave Rivet, was one of Dad's closest friends. Barry had known him since before he could walk.

"Why are we stopping?" Barry asked.

"Dad wants to make sure Uncle Dave is leaving," Mom said.

Uncle Dave had spotted their car through the window. He came outside and hustled over to them, his big belly shaking. Uncle Dave had a smile that made you feel like he'd been waiting his whole life to see you.

Dad stuck his arm out the window. Uncle Dave shook Dad's hand and blew a kiss to Mom. He peered into the backseat.

"Hey there, Barry! Hello there, princess!" he boomed, his words stretched out by his thick drawl.

"Grab your bag," Dad said. "We'll make room for you."

Uncle Dave peered at the little space between Barry and Cleo and laughed.

"You gonna tie me to the roof?" he asked.

But Dad's expression was serious. "They're telling everyone to leave," he said. "That means you too."

"Someone needs to keep an eye on our city!" Uncle Dave said. "I'm keeping the club open so folks have a place to go."

"I don't like it," Dad said.

"This place will be fine," Uncle Dave said. "And so will I."

Barry could tell that Uncle Dave wasn't changing his mind.

Dad grabbed Uncle Dave's hand again.

"You take care," Dad said.

"And if you change your mind, I'm right here," Uncle Dave said. "I already told some folks, 'Don't go to the Superdome. Just come to Lightning's.' I have my generator and about a million hot dogs."

"We'll keep that in mind," Dad said.

Uncle Dave put his hands on Dad's shoulders. "And I better see you this Thursday for the show!"

Dad laughed and started up the engine. "Let's hope!"

"Isn't it a bad idea for him to stay?" Barry asked once they'd driven away.

"This neighborhood doesn't usually get flooded," Dad said. "It's a bit higher than the rest of the city."

"And let's face it: If anyone can keep a hurricane away, it's Dave," Mom said.

They sped toward Interstate 10, but the closer

they got, the heavier the traffic became. Soon their car was standing still.

Barry opened his window and stuck his head out. The line of cars and trucks stretched as far as he could see. The hot and sticky air stunk of car exhaust.

Dad clicked on the radio and punched the buttons until he found a traffic report. The news was terrible: Cars were backed up for hundreds of miles on roads leading out of the city.

"This will take all day," Mom said softly, reaching into the cooler and taking out a blueberry muffin.

Dad patted her leg.

Cleo fussed, and Barry tried to distract her with one of his stories.

An hour went by, and the car didn't budge. Dad had to turn off the air conditioner so the engine wouldn't overheat.

Cleo whined and moaned and finally fell asleep.

Another hour passed. They'd moved just a few feet. Barry's shirt was soaked with sweat.

At this rate it would be hours before they even got onto the highway. And then they had more than three hundred miles to drive.

What if they were stuck in traffic when the storm hit?

Before Barry could ask that scary question, Cleo woke up and started to wail.

And then, as Barry was reaching for her favorite stuffed poodle, a wave of warm soup splashed across his lap. *What in the . . .*

Except it wasn't soup.

Cleo had thrown up. She threw up again, this time into the front seat. And again, onto the floor.

There was a moment of shocked silence, and then Cleo burst into tears.

"Waaaaahhhhhhhhh!" she wailed.

The awful smell rose in the car. Barry put his

hands over his face, which made Cleo scream more.

Mom unhooked her seat belt and scrambled into the backseat. Dad rummaged in the glove compartment and found a wad of napkins. Mom started to wipe off Cleo's face.

"This little girl is burning up!" Mom said.

Barry reached over to feel Cleo's forehead. She was boiling!

"What's wrong?" Barry asked, his heart racing.

"I'm sure she just has a bug," Dad said. "She'll be all right."

Mom gave Cleo a sip of water. "It's okay, baby," she said. "Just try to settle down. You'll feel better soon. . . ."

But Cleo threw up again, and again. She screamed so loudly people in the other lanes peered out their car windows.

Mom and Dad looked at each other, and Barry understood exactly what they were thinking:

There was no way they could get on the highway with Cleo that sick.

Sure enough, Dad pulled out of the line of traffic and pointed the car back toward home.

CHAPTER 7

Cleo threw up all day. Barry tried to help keep her calm, but even he couldn't get her to stop crying. Mom managed to talk to their doctor, who had evacuated to Baton Rouge. He said there was a bad flu going around and Cleo wouldn't start to feel better for at least another day.

Mom and Dad talked about going to the Superdome. But the newscaster on TV said there were already ten thousand people at the football stadium, with thousands more lined up around the building.

"We're hearing there is not enough food or water at the Dome," the newscaster said. "And if the power goes off, it's going to be like an oven in there."

Then they showed a man who had been turned away because he wanted to bring his little dog with him.

"They say no pets," the man said, holding the dog up to the camera. "But I can't leave this guy all by himself!"

Looking at those crowds on television, Barry was relieved when Mom and Dad decided they were better off at home.

Throughout the afternoon, Barry kept his eyes on the sky. By six o'clock, the wind had kicked up. The sky turned gray with streaks of silver. But the strangest thing was the silence. Their block was deserted. There were no motorcycles *vroom*ing. No kids laughing and shouting. No music playing or basketballs bouncing. Usually the trees were filled with birds, and frogs chirped from the bushes. But there wasn't a bird in sight, and not a peep was to be heard.

And then, around ten o'clock that night, the wind and rain started for real.

Dad and Barry were settled on the living room couch. The baseball playoffs were on, and Dad had set them up with a feast of chips, salsa, and sodas. Mom and Cleo were fast asleep in Mom and Dad's room.

The wind moaned at first. Then it started to howl, and finally it was shrieking so loudly Dad had to turn up the TV. Barry moved closer to Dad.

Soon there were other noises.

Pom, pom, pom.

"That's just the rain banging against the metal roof on the shed," Dad said.

Ka-bang!

"Whoops, a gutter came loose."

Che-chong!

"There goes part of someone's fence."

Dad sat there calmly, watching the game, munching on chips. Barry remembered their plane ride to New York the past summer. An hour into the flight, they had flown into a thunderstorm. How that airplane bounced up and down! It felt like a giant hand was dribbling the plane like a basketball. Flashes of lightning exploded in the sky. A woman sitting across from Barry burst into tears. The pilot made everyone sit down, even the stewardesses. The plane rattled so badly Barry was sure one of the wings would fall off.

And in all that commotion, Dad had just sat there, reading his book. A few times he'd patted Barry's leg.

"Quite a ride," he'd said, never taking his eyes from the book, never once looking outside at the lightning or craning his neck to see the scared expressions on the stewardesses' faces.

So Barry had kept his eyes glued to Dad's face.

As long as Dad was calm, he decided, he didn't have to worry.

Finally the bouncing stopped. The plane flew out of the clouds and into the clear blue sky.

Later, when they were in a taxi heading into the city, Barry asked Dad how he had stayed so calm. "What were you thinking about?"

"'Blueberry Hill.'"

Barry gave Dad a funny look.

"When I get nervous, I play the song 'Blueberry Hill' in my mind."

Barry knew the song. It was a hit by Fats Domino, the most famous citizen of the Lower Nine. Fats had struck it rich singing songs way before Dad was born. But he never moved out of the neighborhood. Barry and Jay loved to walk by his bright yellow house. Sometimes Fats was out on his porch to wave hello.

Barry watched Dad now as the wind howled and moaned and shrieked.

"Hey, Dad," Barry said, "are you playing 'Blueberry Hill' in your mind?"

Dad laughed.

He put his arm around Barry and pulled him close.

"Nah, I was thinking that wind is making a pretty song."

"Sounds like wolves," Barry said.

"Nah," Dad said.

"Ghosts," Barry said.

"Don't think so," Dad said, listening more closely, tilting his head and half closing his eyes.

Dad clicked off the TV. He reached over and grabbed his trumpet, which he always kept nearby.

The wind shrieked a high note. Dad put his trumpet to his lips and played along.

The wind shifted lower, and so did Dad.

He played softly, along with the wind, until after a while that wind didn't seem so scary, and it actually sounded like a song. Not as pretty as

'Blueberry Hill,' but still a song. Barry almost smiled, imagining Cleo's big fat lady in the sky. Not a vampire, but a pretty singer, belting out her song.

The house shook and rattled, but as Dad's music filled the air, Barry started to feel safe. The lights were bright. Mom and Cleo were cozy in bed. He thought of Gramps patting the walls of the house. In a few hours the sky would turn blue again.

Barry had planned to stay up with Dad, to help him keep an eye out for leaks, to watch over Cleo and Mom. But now he felt tired. All the late nights he'd stayed up working on Akivo . . . and all today he'd been so worried about Clee. . . . Maybe he could take a little rest, catnap like Mom did after dinner, before she started her hours of baking.

Barry closed his eyes . . . drifting, drifting, drifting . . .

And then his eyes popped open.

It took Barry a minute to understand that he had fallen asleep. The room was dark except for the flickering light of a candle on the corner table. The power must have gone out. He squinted at his watch: 6:35. It was morning! He'd slept for hours.

And what had woken him up?

A noise. Not the wind, which was still shrieking and moaning. Not the rain, which hammered down even harder than when Barry had closed his eyes. No. There was a new noise out there. A kind of *whoosh*ing sound.

Barry sat up.

Dad's coffee mug, half empty, sat on the floor. Where was Dad? Was Cleo okay? And what was that strange noise that had woken Barry up?

Barry heard Dad's footsteps upstairs. He stood up, but before he could take two steps, the front door flew open.

A wave of water swept into the house. It

swirled around Barry's legs, knocking him off his feet.

There was a scream, but this time it wasn't the wind.

It was Barry.

CHAPTER 8

"Barry! Barry!"

Dad was pounding down the stairs. He splashed through the water, grabbed Barry by the arm, lifting him up, and pulled him toward the staircase. Furniture and other objects floated around them like bath toys—the new couch Mom had saved for a year to buy, the little square lamp table where Gramps used to play chess, framed pictures of Barry and Cleo from school. The water was rising fast! It was up to Barry's waist by the time they reached the stairs — and it kept getting higher. It was like their house was a bucket being filled up by the biggest hose in the world.

Where was all this water coming from? The water in Gramps's stories hadn't been this wild.

Mom burst out of her room with Cleo in her arms as Dad and Barry made it to the top of the staircase.

She looked down the stairs and gasped. She wrapped her free arm around Barry, pulling him close.

"The levee, Roddy," she said to Dad.

"The levee broke?" Barry asked, picturing the Industrial Canal. The canal was five miles long and very deep. Was all that water pouring into their neighborhood?

Mom and Dad seemed frozen, staring at the rising water.

Panic boiled up inside Barry.

"What will happen?" Barry asked. "What

will we do? What . . ." His voice trailed off. He wasn't even sure he wanted to know the answers to his questions.

They all stood there, huddled together, watching the water move up the stairs.

"We need to go up to the attic," Dad said. "Now."

Dad pulled open the hatch in the ceiling and a blast of hot air came down. Barry had been up there only once in his life. It was a tiny space, dark and hot like an oven, with a ceiling that sloped down so you couldn't stand up straight.

Cleo started to cry.

"No!" she yelled. She tried to run away. "No go up!"

Dad caught her. "Cleo!" he said. She struggled to escape, screaming and squirming. There was no way they could force her up the rickety stairs.

"It's all right," Barry said, taking hold of his sister's hand.

"No! No!" she insisted.

"Clee," he said, working hard to keep his voice steady, "Akivo might be up there."

Cleo sniffed. She let Barry pick her up, and put her arms around his neck. She buried her head in his chest. She still felt feverish. He held her more tightly.

Dad sent Mom up first. Then Barry put Cleo on the ladder and climbed up right behind her. Dad came up last, and they all sat down together in the darkness. There was barely enough room for the four of them, and they were squashed together. The air was so hot it burned Barry's lungs. It stunk like mildew and dust.

He tried not to imagine what was happening just below the attic floor: every single thing they owned—their furniture, Cleo's toys, Mom's cookbooks, Dad's trumpet and all his music— being covered with water.

And Akivo.

He was trapped in Barry's room somewhere.

Lost.

For the past few weeks, thinking about Akivo had given Barry the feeling—a secret, happy feeling—that maybe he wasn't really the scared little kid he saw in the bathroom mirror. He and Jay had created something unique, something special. Somehow, the bright colors of Barry's drawing seemed to have gotten inside him.

But now the bright and powerful feeling drained away. With every minute that ticked by, Barry felt more helpless and terrified. Cleo was whimpering again. Mom held her on her lap, rocking back and forth, singing softly to calm her.

The water was rising past the second floor. They could hear the *whoosh*ing and *bang*ing of furniture below.

What would they do? Where could they go?

Barry's whole body was shaking.

His mind was spinning.

And then Dad leaned in closer.

He put one hand on Barry's shoulder and the other on Mom's.

"I want you to listen carefully," he said softly. "We are all together. And as long as we're all together, we are going to come through this."

Even in the darkness, Barry could see Dad's eyes blazing.

"Soon this will be over," Dad said. "We just have to get through the next few hours."

Mom wiped away Barry's tears.

"We can't stay here in the attic," Dad said. "We're going up onto the roof."

Mom's eyes got wider. She swallowed. "All right," she said.

"But there's no way out," Barry said.

"Yes, there is," Dad said.

"How?" Barry asked.

"Your grandfather."

Barry stared at Dad. Gramps had died three years earlier. Dad wasn't the kind who believed in angels flying around. What was he talking about?

Dad crawled to the darkest corner of the attic. He started back with what looked like a stick.

As he got closer, Barry saw what it was: an ax.

"Gramps always said there'd be another bad storm," Dad said. "He kept this ax up here for forty years. And he made sure I knew about it."

It took Barry a minute to realize what Dad was going to do with that ax.

"Keep your heads down," Dad said.

Mom pulled Barry and Cleo to her.

Dad heaved the ax over his shoulder. With a mighty swing, he smashed the blade into the ceiling.

CHAPTER 9

The water had risen to the attic by the time Dad chopped a hole big enough for them to climb through. The wind screamed and rain poured in.

"Stay together," Dad shouted. "We're going to stay together."

Cleo was so stunned that she stopped fussing. She kept her eyes on Barry's face, and he did his best to look calm, like Dad on the plane.

Dad dragged a trunk under the hole, stepped onto it, and pulled himself onto the roof.

"Barry!" Dad yelled. "Climb up."

Barry stood on the trunk. Dad lifted him by the arms, and Mom grabbed his legs, pushing him up slowly.

Barry gasped when he stuck his head into the storm. The wind was so strong he couldn't keep his eyes open. The rain came down hard and fast, stinging his face like a million bees. Dad held on to Barry, then helped him lie down on his stomach. The wind pushed against Barry's back, gluing him to the roof.

"Stay there!" Dad shouted.

Cleo came up next. Dad laid her down next to Barry. Barry put his arm around her and held on. Soon Barry and Cleo were sandwiched tightly between Mom and Dad.

They lay bundled together like that, not talking. Mom had her arm over Barry's head. Dad's hand rested on his back. Cleo was pushed so close against Barry he could feel her heart beating. He smelled Mom's lemony soap.

Barry kept his eyes closed. But just as he started to feel a tiny bit calmer, there was a loud thud at the end of the roof.

Something had blown through the air and smacked against the house.

Cleo sprang up, struggling to her feet, breaking free from Mom's and Dad's hold.

"Akivo?" she called.

The wind knocked her forward. Mom screamed.

Barry's hand shot out and grabbed Cleo by the back of her shirt. Dad got a grip on her arm. They pulled her back into their huddle.

Barry's heart hammered.

They got Cleo to lie flat again. But before Barry could rejoin their huddle, a gust of wind swirled around him and hit him in the chest. He tumbled onto his side.

"Barry!" Dad called, holding out his hand.

Barry reached out, expecting to feel Dad's grip.

But he slipped back, and his hand sliced through empty air.

He slid down.

Down.

Down.

Down.

The last thing he saw before he fell into the water was the terrified look on Dad's face.

CHAPTER 10

The water seemed to reach up and snatch Barry out of the air. And then he was swept away in a gushing tide. Barry struggled to keep his face above the waves, to keep water from rushing into his nose and mouth. His leg smacked into a piece of wood, but that barely slowed him down. His arm scraped against something sharp. His hand hit something big and furry—a rat?—as the water twisted and turned him and dragged him along.

And then, finally—*crash*—he hit something that stopped him cold.

It was a tree. Almost without thinking, Barry threw his arms around the trunk. The water pulled him, trying to suck him back into the flood. But he held on. He wrapped one leg around the tree, then the other. He hugged that tree so tightly he could barely breathe.

He gathered his strength and then he managed to shinny up the trunk inch by inch. It was an oak tree. All of the branches had been ripped away but one, which rose out of the water. Barry pulled himself up onto it and sat in the V where the branch met the trunk. He hugged the trunk again, bracing himself against the wind.

He couldn't see much in the gray light and the stinging rain. And what he saw hardly seemed real: water in every direction. He felt like he was shipwrecked in the middle of the ocean.

The water was filled with branches and wooden boards and other wreckage from the storm. Barry thought of Atlantis, a city lost under the ocean. He'd read about it in one of his favorite comic books.

Was that what would become of New Orleans?

Barry pressed his cheek against the tree. His entire body ached. His hands were ragged from climbing the tree. He started to cry, his sounds drowned out by the wind.

"Dad!" Barry screamed. "Mom! Cleo!"

He screamed their names until his throat burned.

The wind screamed back at him.

And then he heard a deep groan and a *crack* that echoed above the wind.

A massive shadow loomed over him.

Barry stared in shock: It was a house, pushing through the water like a monster. The windows and doors were gone, and as the house turned slowly in the water, Barry saw that one side had been ripped away.

He had to get out of the way. Now!

Barry jumped into the water, barely missing a big piece of glass. The house hit the tree with a *smash* and a groan and then got stuck there. The current started to drag Barry. He fought against it and somehow managed to swim to the house. He reached up and grabbed hold of a window frame, careful of the jagged glass around the edge.

A piece of wood fell into the water right next to Barry.

Its bright color glowed in the ghostly light: sky blue.

Barry stared at the house.

Could it be?

Yes. It was Abe's house. Abe Mackay's.

And that wasn't all.

The sound of ferocious barking rang out.

Somewhere in that ripped-apart house was Cruz.

The killer dog.

CHAPTER 11

Barry's heart pounded.

That dog was crazy. What if he came after Barry?

Cruz barked some more.

Barry had to get out of here!

But then there was a noise—a whimpering howl. It rose above the wind, and it was the saddest sound Barry had ever heard. Sadder than Cleo's sobbing. Sadder than the song Dad had played at Gramps's funeral. Sadder than Barry's own sobs.

That didn't sound like a killer dog.

It sounded like a dog that was terrified.

Cruz howled again.

Begging. Pleading.

Help me, please, he seemed to be saying. *Help me, please.*

Barry knew what he had to do.

He hoisted himself up, climbed through the window, and eased himself down on the other side. It was very dark, but Barry could see shadowy shapes around him: a couch floating in the corner, a smashed lamp, and a big cabinet lying facedown in the water.

Cruz barked brightly, like he could tell help was on the way.

"Cruz!" Barry shouted.

The dog barked again.

"I'm coming!" Barry called.

Barry waded carefully. His shoes were still floating around in his living room at home; his socks had been ripped off in his ride through the flood. Already his feet were sliced up, and he knew there had to be glass and nails everywhere.

Cruz was whimpering loudly now.

"Don't worry!" Barry called.

Cruz barked like he understood.

Barry made it to the stairway, which rose out of the water. The house was tilted to the side and rocked gently in the waves. Barry had to hold on tightly to the banister.

Cruz was waiting for him in the doorway of Abe's room. His leash was attached to Abe's bed, which Cruz had managed to drag across the room. He was straining so hard to get free that he was practically strangling himself.

Barry paused for a second, thinking of all the scary stories Abe had told him about Cruz. But then he closed his eyes and swallowed hard.

He walked up, reached for Cruz's collar, and unhooked it from the leash.

Cruz leaped up, and for a split second Barry thought he'd made a terrible mistake.

But then Cruz licked Barry's chin. He licked Barry's hands and pushed his head against Barry's leg. Then he sat down and looked up into Barry's eyes. He gave four little barks.

Thank you! he seemed to cheer. *Thank you! Thank you! Thank you!*

Barry bent down next to Cruz and patted him on the head.

"You're welcome," he said.

Cruz gave Barry one last kiss on the nose and then looked at him expectantly.

What now? he seemed to ask. *What should we do?*

And that was when it hit Barry: He wasn't alone anymore. He and Cruz were together.

CHAPTER 12

The back wall of Abe's room was gone. But there was a spot near the top of the stairs where they could escape from the wind and rain. Barry and Cruz sat there for a few minutes, until Cruz started to whimper.

"What's wrong?" Barry asked.

The dog was panting.

"You thirsty? You need water?"

Cruz's tail thumped.

Barry knew that none of the sinks would

work. But maybe there were bottles of water somewhere in the kitchen.

Barry and Cruz made their way down the slanting staircase.

"You stay here," Barry said to Cruz, pointing to the bottom of the stairs. He didn't want Cruz wading through the dirty water.

But Cruz wouldn't stay. He seemed to be glued to Barry's leg.

They waded into the small kitchen. Dishes were floating around their feet, along with boxes and cans of food, but nothing to drink.

Barry yanked open the fridge, and a thrill went through him when he saw two six-packs of Coke, some cheese, hot dogs, bread, and a large bottle of water.

"We're in luck," he said to Cruz.

He looked around for something to carry the food in. He saw a plastic bag floating in the corner and bent down to reach for it. But before he could grab it, Cruz let out a ferocious bark and rammed his body against Barry, almost knocking him down.

A long, dark shape shot out from under the bag and disappeared into the murky water.

A snake!

Barry stood still, frozen in fear.

Was that a water moccasin?

He remembered Gramps's most terrifying Betsy story, about one of his friends who'd been bitten by a water moccasin while making his way through the flooded streets.

"The water was filled with poisonous snakes," Gramps had said. "Lots of people got bit."

Now Barry shuddered.

He grabbed as much food and soda and water as he could carry. He hurried back upstairs, praying that snakes couldn't climb.

There was a metal bowl in Abe's room, and Barry filled it to the top. Cruz emptied it, and Barry filled it up again. Barry drank two cans of Coke. He ripped open the package of hot dogs;

Cruz ate four, one after another. Barry made himself a cheese sandwich and gave Cruz the crusts.

When they were finished, they settled back against the wall. Cruz lay down on top of Barry's legs. He looked up at Barry with a *thank you* kind of look on his face.

Barry stroked his head.

"You're really not a killer dog, are you?" Barry said.

Cruz looked at him and panted a little. Nah. That dog was probably from the shelter in downtown New Orleans. Abe couldn't afford a fancy Chinese army dog even if he'd wanted one. He had made up that killer-dog routine. Another trick to scare the bejesus out of Barry and Jay.

"The storm will be over soon," Barry said to Cruz.

The wind seemed to be dying down a bit.

Cruz was still looking up at him. Barry saw the fear and confusion in his eyes.

What could Barry do?

And then it came to him.

"I found my thrill," Barry sang quietly, "on Blueberry Hill . . ."

Cruz licked Barry's chin. He liked it.

So Barry kept singing—"The moon stood still . . . on Blueberry Hill"—until Cruz put his head on Barry's knee and closed his eyes.

Soon Barry's eyelids started to sag. He stopped singing and leaned back to take a rest, lulled by the gentle rocking of the house and by the song—familiar now—of Katrina's winds and rain.

CHAPTER 13

Cruz was barking. Barking like crazy.

Barry shook himself awake.

Cruz was standing at the edge of the room, where the side of the house had been ripped away. But he was looking back at Barry as he barked.

Come! he seemed to be saying. *Come here and look!*

Something thundered in the sky. The house was shuddering and rocking.

What was happening?

Was it a tornado? An earthquake?

No! It was a helicopter!

It hovered low in the sky, its winds churning the floodwater.

Barry could see the pilot, a young man, through the windshield. He seemed to be looking right at Barry.

"Cruz!" Barry exclaimed. "We're being rescued!"

Barry waved at the pilot. "Here!" he said. "Here! We're here!"

It's over! Barry thought. They'd made it! Soon they'd be out of the flood! He'd be back with Mom and Dad and Cleo!

Barry waved his arms.

The helicopter hovered for a minute longer.

But then it suddenly rose and flew away.

Was it circling? Was it going to come around the other side?

Barry waited. And waited. But the helicopter's

sound grew fainter, and then it faded away completely.

"No!" Barry shouted. "Come back!"

Cruz looked at him, confused.

Barry felt like crying. But he wanted to be strong. For Cruz.

"I'm sorry," Barry said as calmly as he could. "I thought they were coming for us."

The helicopter's winds had stirred up the water, and now the house was rocking so violently that Barry was knocked onto his knees. Cruz yelped. Before Barry could pick himself up, he heard a loud splash.

Cruz had fallen into the water!

Barry dove toward the open side of the house and peered over the edge.

He searched for Cruz, but all he could see was a mess of wood planks and branches. Something poked up in the middle of the debris but then disappeared. It was Cruz! He was tangled up in the mess and struggling to keep his head above the water.

Barry fought the urge to jump right in. It was a ten-foot drop at least. And he had to be careful not to hit anything sharp floating in the water.

"I'm coming, Cruz!" Barry yelled as he eased himself over the side of the house, holding tightly with his hands while letting his legs drop.

He dangled there for a minute, grasping

the edge, staring down into the water, until he spotted a big board floating underneath. Just as it passed, Barry let go. He hit the waves but grabbed hold of the wood before his head went under. He pulled his body onto the board and kicked over to Cruz. The dog was trapped between two branches.

Barry pulled away the biggest branch and grabbed Cruz by the collar.

"I have you," he said, pulling the dog close, hooking his arm around Cruz's body.

Cruz licked him on the cheek and pushed his nose into Barry's ear like he wanted to whisper a secret.

"I know," Barry said. "That was scary. But we're okay. We're okay."

But they weren't okay.

The water was burning Barry's skin. The fumes stung his eyes. Cruz had to be suffering too. They couldn't go back to Abe's broken house. Barry wouldn't be able to lift Cruz through the window. And they couldn't just float like this either.

In the distance, Barry saw the rooftop of a house poking through the water. It was too far to swim to through the poisonous flood. And then he saw a car floating toward them. It was upside down, like a turtle flipped onto its back. Maybe he and Cruz could ride the car to the roof of that house.

Barry kicked as hard as he could, holding Cruz with one hand and the board with the other. They made it to the car and scrambled up onto it. Barry held on to one of the tires, and Cruz stayed close to him. Slowly, the car moved toward the house, almost as though they were driving it. When they were a few feet away, Barry stood up, balancing himself, ready to jump.

"Come on!" he said to Cruz.

And they both leaped off the car and onto the roof.

Cruz slipped, but this time Barry grabbed him

before he fell. They staggered up to a small dry patch near the top of the roof.

Barry sat down, pulling Cruz onto his lap.

He suddenly felt more tired than he'd ever felt in his life. He rested his chin on Cruz's head. Barry could hear dogs barking and howling all around them. He remembered the news report that had said no one could bring pets to the Superdome. There must be hundreds of dogs and cats on their own. Thousands.

And people too. In the distance Barry could hear voices calling for help. He and Cruz weren't the only ones out here.

The light drained from the sky and the sun went down. Barry and Cruz sat slumped together. Neither of them moved. Barry was thirsty but there was no water to drink. Mosquitoes swarmed around them, too many to swat away.

There was nothing to do.

And there was nowhere to go.

CHAPTER 14

The stars came out, more stars than Barry had ever imagined.

Was one of them Beta Draconis, Akivo's secret star?

Beta Draconis was a real star. Barry and Jay had found the name in an astronomy book in the library. They'd learned that there were trillions and trillions of stars in the universe, more stars than grains of sand on every beach and desert on earth. They all seemed to be out that night.

Barry searched the sky and picked out one of the very brightest stars.

"See that, Cruz?" he whispered, pointing into the sky. "That's Akivo's star."

That probably wasn't true. But right then, Barry decided to believe it.

Cruz looked at the sky, and his brown eyes filled up with light. He and Barry leaned their heads together. And soon the sky seemed to wrap itself around them, a glittering blanket to protect them from the awful sights and sounds and smells of their ruined neighborhood.

They sat like that for hours on their little dry patch of roof. A few small boats motored by. Barry called out, but nobody seemed to hear him.

Until, finally, one of the boats slowed down.

It wasn't really a boat. It was more like a raft. A yellow rubber raft with a motor.

The driver was a woman, younger than Mom. She drove the boat right onto the roof and stopped it just a few feet from Barry and Cruz.

"Well, look at you, brave soul," the woman said, her voice low and smooth.

She had very dark skin and huge eyes and dozens of long, skinny braids that seemed to dance around her face. Barry stared at her, sure he was imagining things. She seemed like some kind of fairy—a beautiful fairy in a yellow rubber boat—from one of Cleo's bedtime stories.

But she was real, stepping out of her boat and wading up to Barry in tall rubber boots.

She put a hand on Cruz's head. The dog didn't growl. Like Barry, he seemed hypnotized.

"Who are you?" the woman asked.

Barry's throat was dry and swollen. But he managed to say his name.

"I'm Nell," she said. "Where's your family?"

Barry looked around him at the endless water. His eyes filled with tears.

Nell put her hands on Barry's shoulders.

"How about we get you and your friend out of here?" she asked. "Sound like a plan?"

Barry wiped his eyes and somehow choked out the word "yes."

Barry and Cruz climbed into the boat after Nell.

Nell handed Barry a big bottle of water. She filled a cup for Cruz and held it while he lapped the water up. Barry gulped down his water, almost choking at first. When he was finished, he took a deep breath. He opened his mouth to say thank you, but the only sound that came out was a sob. Suddenly tears were pouring down his face.

He turned away from Nell.

She had called him a brave soul. So why couldn't he act brave?

He was finally off that roof. But now all the terror he'd felt those past hours came back to him, second by second. He felt as if he was

shrinking, as though his fear was boiling up inside him and he was melting away.

"We're going to the St. Claude Avenue Bridge," Nell said. "There will be people to help you there."

Of course there would be. Police and firemen. Doctors and nurses. Barry knew what happened in disasters. He'd seen it on the news. He imagined a big tent on the bridge, with cots set up in neat rows. He would get fresh clothes, more water, good food. The people there would know how to track down Mom and Dad and Cleo.

Barry took a deep breath.

Nell carefully wove the little boat through the maze of uprooted trees and wreckage. People stranded on rooftops called to them as they rode by.

"Help us!"

"We've got a baby here!"

"We're hurt! Please help!"

Nell called back to all of them.

"I'll be back!" she said over and over. "Hang on there! I'll be back."

She whispered a prayer under her breath.

"There are thousands of people stranded, just here in the Lower Nine," Nell said to Barry. "I've already picked up more than thirty people."

Finally the bridge appeared in the distance.

And even from far away, Barry could see that

there were no tents. No flashing lights or police cars or fire engines or ambulances.

Other boats — little boats, like Nell's — pulled up to the bridge, let people off, and then headed back out into the water. There were at least a hundred people packed on the bridge. Families huddled together; old couples sat on the ground; people walked around dazed.

Was Nell really going to leave Barry there by himself?

CHAPTER 15

Nell eased the boat onto the ramp that led to the bridge. Part of the bridge was underwater, but the middle part was high enough that it had stayed dry.

Nell switched off the engine.

"You'll be okay here," she said. "They're bringing people to the Superdome. Someone will help you there."

Barry wanted to believe her. But he knew that even before the storm hit, there had been huge crowds. And not enough food or water. What would it be like now?

And besides, they wouldn't let him in with Cruz.

Barry's fear started to boil up again.

A man came running over.

"Pardon me," he said to Nell, breathing hard. "I'm trying to find my grandmother. She's out there, all alone, up on her roof. I need to get to her, I need . . ."

"I'll take you," Nell said.

The man nodded, wiping away a tear.

"Thank you," he whispered. "Thank you."

Barry knew he had to get out of the boat. Nell had other people to help, like she'd helped him.

Nell leaned over and put her hand under Barry's chin, lifting his face so he had to look at her.

She didn't say anything for a moment. She just looked into his eyes, like she saw something there worth looking at.

"You're strong," she said with no doubt in her voice.

Barry didn't feel strong. His whole body shook as he got out of the boat.

Cruz followed him. They stood on the ramp and watched as the man pushed the boat into deeper water. He climbed in beside Nell.

Nell nodded at Barry, and he suddenly had the idea he'd never see her again. She powered up her engine and the boat pulled away.

As Barry watched Nell disappear, her words echoed through his mind.

You're strong. You're strong.

And soon it wasn't Nell's voice he was hearing in his mind.

It was his own voice.

I am strong. I am strong.

Was he?

He was scared. He was standing there crying, his legs quivering like skinny little twigs in the wind.

But did that mean he wasn't strong?

Barry thought about what had happened to him. How he'd been swept off the roof and carried away. How he'd grabbed hold of that tree and climbed up. How he'd held on tightly against the wind and the rain. How he'd saved Cruz. How they'd made their way through the wreckage to that tiny dry patch of roof.

He'd felt scared the entire time.

But here he was, standing on dry ground. In one piece.

He looked up, and there was his bright star.

Barry's star.

And right then he knew that no matter how scared he felt, he'd find his way.

Or someone would find him.

An hour passed, and Barry heard a familiar voice.

"Barry! Barry!"

And then other voices, calling his name, together, like a song.

Dad reached him first. Then Mom and Cleo.

Their arms wrapped around Barry.

And they stood there together for a long time.

The four Tuckers and Cruz, a tiny island in a huge sea.

CHAPTER 16

SATURDAY, SEPTEMBER 29, 2005
RIVERSIDE PARK, NEW YORK CITY

Barry sat on a bench in the shade. Mom and Dad were standing a few feet away, watching Cleo climb up the jungle gym. Cruz was snoozing at Barry's feet. Barry had a sketchbook open on his lap, and he was looking at his new drawing of Akivo. He'd finished that morning, keeping his promise to Jay. It had been Jay's idea that they could still enter the contest. Jay had even called the Acclaim offices from his grandma's house in Birmingham.

"I told them the whole story," he said. "The man said we can still enter. And they want to meet you!"

Barry wasn't surprised to hear that.

Even four weeks later, Katrina was the biggest story in the country. Every time Barry turned on the TV or got into a taxi with Mom or Dad, another voice was talking about the hurricane.

"This is the worst disaster ever to hit America."

"This is a national tragedy."

"A great American city has been destroyed."

And everyone wanted to hear their story.

The kids at Barry's new school. The man who made their sandwiches at the deli on the corner. Strangers who overheard Mom talking at the bank. They all wanted to know about Katrina. They listened with wide eyes. And then they all

said pretty much the same thing: They said the Tuckers were lucky.

Barry knew that was true.

Mom said it was a miracle that they'd found Barry on the bridge. Some families had been separated for days or weeks. Some still hadn't found each other.

And of course there were people who had died — more than a thousand. They were still finding bodies in attics.

Barry had nightmares about the storm. He didn't sleep much. Even the sound of Dad turning on the shower in the morning made Barry's heart jump.

But yes, he knew he was lucky.

Luckier than the tens of thousands of people who'd been stranded for days in the hot and terrifying Superdome. Or the people who'd been stuck on bridges and highways and rooftops.

The Tuckers hadn't gone to the Superdome.

They had gone to Lightning's. They'd stayed with Dave for two days and then caught a bus to Houston. Dave boarded up the club and went to Baton Rouge. By then even he realized that the city wasn't safe.

The cousins in Houston spoiled them rotten for one week. Mom and Dad talked about moving there, finding an apartment nearby. But then a call came from the president of that famous music college in New York. There was a job for Dad if he wanted, teaching about New Orleans music. There was an apartment too, with furniture and room for the whole family.

A week later, they were here.

Cruz too. He was part of the family now. The Red Cross had helped Dad track down Abe and his grandma in Little Rock, Arkansas. Abe and Barry had talked on the phone. And Abe—the old Abe—had asked Barry if he would keep Cruz.

"He's not a killer," Abe said.

"I figured that out."

They had a good laugh.

And they cried a little too, when they talked about their neighborhood.

Barry hoped he would see Abe again one day.

Mom and Dad came over and sat next to Barry on the bench. Cleo waved from the top of the slide.

Dad looked at Barry's drawing of Akivo.

"That is really something," Dad said.

"Thanks," said Barry, who liked this one even better than the original. Akivo had a sidekick now, a mutt with floppy ears. And he had a guardian angel—a beautiful fairy in a yellow rubber raft.

"He looks like you," Mom said.

"That's right," Dad said. "I see it too."

Barry stared at the picture, and he saw what Mom and Dad meant. Akivo's face—it did look something like Barry's.

"I guess you feel a little like a superhero yourself," Mom said.

"Nah," Barry said, his cheeks heating up.

But really, he did.

Out there in the flood, Barry had discovered some powers of his own.

When it was time to go back to the apartment, Barry went to pluck Cleo off the jungle gym. He heard her singing, "On Blueberry Hill . . . ," and he smiled. Dad told Barry he'd sung that song a million times when they'd been on the roof. Dad had jumped into the floodwater after Barry, but the current had been too strong. He'd fought his way back to Mom and Cleo. The three of them had waited out the storm. Mom said that Dad had called Barry's name so many times that he'd lost his voice.

They walked back to Broadway, Barry pushing Cleo in her stroller.

Mom pointed out a bakery with a HELP WANTED

sign in the window. Dad said they should go to the Bronx Zoo later. Or the American Museum of Natural History.

"There's so much to see," Mom said.

"We have plenty of time," Dad said.

It was true. They had time.

But not forever.

Barry knew they would go back to New Orleans, where they belonged.

When would that be?

When would their city be healed?

Barry didn't ask Mom and Dad those questions.

He already knew the answer.

One day.

One day.

AFTER THE STORM:
QUESTIONS ABOUT KATRINA

For many years before Hurricane Katrina, experts had warned that levees in New Orleans were not strong enough to withstand a powerful hurricane. In August 2005, their worst predictions came true. Katrina's 125-mile-per-hour winds sent a gigantic wave of water from the Gulf of Mexico into the canals and lakes surrounding New Orleans. All of that water pushed up against the levees, and many of them failed, some crumbling like the walls of sandcastles. Billions of gallons of water gushed into New Orleans.

Nearly 1,000 people drowned in the first hours of the flooding. Tens of thousands more were like the Tuckers — caught in a nightmare, struggling to survive as water filled their homes. Thousands of people were rescued from their rooftops and attics, often by volunteers like Nell. Nearly 50,000 were stranded in the Superdome in agonizing heat, without enough food or water. It took five full days for help to arrive, and another week before everyone was evacuated from the city.

In the weeks and months after Katrina, many wondered if the great American city of New Orleans would ever recover. There was so much damage. Tens of thousands of houses were destroyed, as well as schools, hospitals, police stations, roads, and businesses. There was no electricity or clean water, and 80 percent of the city was covered with water filled with toxic chemicals and waste. The city's 440,000 residents were scattered all around the country.

But New Orleans did survive. And years later, it continues to recover — building by building, house by house, tree by tree, road by road, family by family. Seventy-five percent of residents have returned. To many visitors, the city seems as vibrant as it always was, with unforgettable music and food, beautiful buildings and gardens, and streets that bustle with energy unlike any other city in America.

But in some of the poorest and hardest-hit neighborhoods, recovery has been painfully slow. If Barry were to come back to the Lower Ninth Ward today, he would see few of his neighbors smiling down from their porches. Much of the Lower Nine is still abandoned. Only 19 percent of that neighborhood's residents have returned.

I've studied dozens of natural disasters over the years — earthquakes and volcanic eruptions and shipwrecks and blizzards and hurricanes. But none of these events made me feel as sad—or as angry—as I felt reading about the horrifying experiences of those who lived through Katrina. Why didn't our leaders do a better job protecting the beautiful city of New Orleans and its citizens? With so many warnings about the dangers of flooding, why wasn't more done to make the levees stronger? Why was help so slow to arrive to the survivors?

As a writer of fiction, I could give Barry and his family a happy ending. But even after reading everything I could find about this storm, I could not find the answers to these questions.

FACTS ABOUT
HURRICANE KATRINA

- Hurricane Katrina was one of the worst
  disasters to ever strike the United
  States. Millions of people in Louisiana,
  Mississippi, and Alabama lost their
  homes and businesses. The death toll
  reached 1,800, including 1,500 who lost
  their lives in New Orleans.

- More than 340,000 people evacuated
  from New Orleans before the storm hit.
  An estimated 100,000 stayed behind.
  Many of these people were too old or
  sick to easily make the trip. Others
  didn't have cars or couldn't afford
  the costs of evacuation—gas for their
  cars; train, bus, or plane tickets;
  hotel rooms. Some thought the storm
  wouldn't be as bad as predicted.

- Among those who stayed behind was Fats Domino. The famous musician, then seventy-seven years old, was with his family in their home in the Lower Ninth Ward. Like the Tuckers', Domino's house flooded quickly when the Industrial Canal levee failed. Mr. Domino and his family escaped into their attic. They were rescued the next day, and spent the rest of the week at the Superdome before taking a bus to Baton Rouge and finally landing in Texas. His famous yellow house still stands, but it is in ruins.

- Katrina also caused a crisis for the animals of New Orleans. Pets were banned from the Superdome, and after the storm, few people were allowed to bring their pets on buses leaving the city. Tens of thousands of pets were stranded without food and water after the storm.

- In the weeks after the flood, the Humane Society of the United States organized the biggest animal rescue in history. Hundreds of volunteers from all over the country came to New Orleans. They broke into boarded-up houses, plucked dogs and cats from rooftops and trees, and even rescued pigs and goats. Many animals were reunited with their owners. Others were sent to shelters across America to be adopted by new families.

- Americans donated more than $1 billion to help the victims of Hurricane Katrina. Other countries donated too. The largest donor was the government of Kuwait, which gave $500 million.

- Hurricane Katrina was the fiftieth recorded hurricane to pass through Louisiana.

I SURVIVED

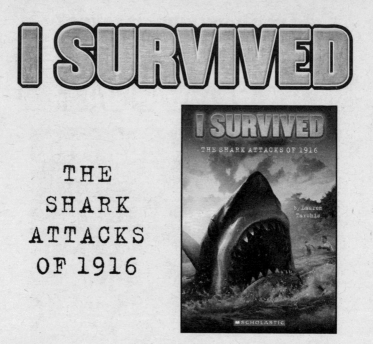

THE SHARK ATTACKS OF 1916

THERE'S SOMETHING IN THE WATER...

Chet Roscow is finally feeling at home in Elm Hills, New Jersey. He has a job with his uncle Jerry at the local diner, three great friends, and the perfect summer-time destination: cool, refreshing Matawan Creek.

But Chet's summer is interrupted by shocking news. A great white shark has been attacking swimmers along the Jersey shore, not far from Elm Hills. Everyone in town is talking about it. So when Chet sees something in the creek, he's sure it's his imagination . . . until he comes face-to-face with a bloodthirsty shark!